GOOD NIGHT, WIGGLY TOES

HIGH**TREE**

P U B L I S H I N G

GOOD NIGHT, WIGGLY TOES

BY RODA AHMED and LEANDRA ROSE · ILLUSTRATED BY FANNY LIEM

THE DAY IS OVER AND IT'S TIME FOR BED.

TIME TO GO TO
BED, MY LOVE.

BUT MY TOES ARE TOO WIGGLY!

LET'S SAY GOOD NIGHT, WIGGLY TOES.

BUT NOW MY FEET WANT TO RUN!

LET'S SAY GOOD NIGHT, RUNNING FEET.

BUT NOW MY LEGS WANT TO JUMP!

LET'S SAY GOOD NIGHT, JUMPING LEGS.

BUT NOW MY HIPS
WANT TO SHAKE!

LET'S SAY GOOD NIGHT,
SHAKING HIPS.

BUT NOW MY HEART
IS DRUMMING LOUD!

GOOD NIGHT,
DRUMMING HEART.

NOW MY HANDS WANT TO CLAP!

GOOD NIGHT, CLAPPING HANDS.

NOW MY THROAT WANTS TO SING!

GOOD NIGHT, SINGING THROAT.

NOW MY TEETH WANT TO CHOMP!

GOOD NIGHT, CHOMPING TEETH.

NOW MY EARS WANT TO LISTEN!

GOOD NIGHT, LISTENING EARS.

BUT MY EYES WANT TO WANDER!

GOOD NIGHT,
WANDERING EYES.

TIME TO SAY GOOD NIGHT TO YOUR WHOLE BODY.

GOOD NIGHT, WIGGLY TOES,
RUNNING FEET,
AND JUMPING LEGS.

GOOD NIGHT,
SHAKING HIPS,
DANCING BELLY,

AND DRUMMING HEART.

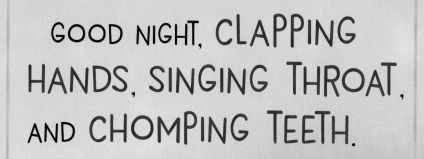

GOOD NIGHT, CLAPPING HANDS, SINGING THROAT, AND CHOMPING TEETH.

GOOD NIGHT, LISTENING EARS AND WANDERING EYES.

GOOD NIGHT, DEAR BODY. THANK YOU FOR CARRYING ME TODAY. NOW, GET SOME SLEEP, AND LET DREAMS DO THE REST.